A BEGINNER'S DREAM SCENE ADVENTURES

A BEGINNER'S DREAM SCENE ADVENTURES

DOREEN LINDAHL

Library of Congress Control Number: 2024925505

First Printing, 2024

CONTENTS

CHAPTER 1

Welcome to My Dream Scene

The power of thought is your ticket to adventure. I have a Dream Scene where I've enjoyed many adventures and you can have Dream Scene adventures, too.

Many years ago, I created my Dream Scene where my imagination takes me on adventures I call 'dreams.' You may call them daydreams, meditations, visualizations, whatever you wish.

I'm going to open the double golden doors to you. After you share my adventures there you will be able to create your own Dream Scene.

A Dream Scene adventure is unplanned. You never know what to expect and every adventure gives you a rest from worries and cares:

Dreaming in Hues of Love

I travel far past time and space
to a special Dream Scene all my own –
a quiet, lovely, peaceful place
that I enjoy when all alone.

What fun to work the magic of imagination
to design special scenes from hues of love
that are unique and wholly mine.

Here I go to ease the pain that pummels
at a tender heart day after day –
and here regain the joy
I had at this life's start.

No sun or moon traverses my sky –
the glow is neither day nor night.
I just enjoy, not asking why,
and beauty fills me with delight.

Again and again, I visit here
to be healed in love's soft gleam.
I love this place...it's very dear,
although I know it's just a dream.

Sometimes I go in with a question and let the dream unfold without any expectations. I may or may not get an answer but it's always a fun adventure.

These dream adventures come from 'somewhere' and I call them gifts. Seek with your heart full of the 'hues of love' and you can have fun adventures, too. Having love for everything in nature is important in both a Dream Scene and in the Awake World where we are now.

I am only the transcriber of these dreams and don't claim any merit they may have. If the dreams lack in any way, as the transcriber I don't claim that lack either. As you share my dreams, you may discover ideas for creating your own Dream Scenes. Already, your adventures are inside you waiting to be found.

You may accept or reject any detail of my dreams and are free to create your Dream Scene in your own original way. I wrote some of my adventures into these scenes to show you one way to have adventures. When you write your dreams down, you can experience them over again and also share them.

You need seven tools for creating a Dream Scene:

- The first five tools are *Sight*, *Hearing*, *Touch*, *Taste* and *Smell*.
- The sixth tool is *Imagination*.
- The seventh tool is *Fun*. You can gain important insights when you visit your Dream Scene in a spirit of fun.

Get Ready for Your Adventure

Sit relaxed on a chair or lean against a bank of pillows. Breathe deeply of the hues of love three times and relax. Let all your muscles soften, beginning with your head and neck. As tension flows away, gently melt into peaceful quietness.

Close your eyes. Come with me to the bottom of a grassy hill. A white mist hides the top of the hill. Push open the double golden doors in the mist.

Your Dream Scene Adventure will now begin.

CHAPTER 2

A Yellow Butterfly Dream

I stood at the foot of the grassy hill. A red-tailed hawk in summer splendor circled overhead than banked and disappeared into the mist on top of the hill.

The grass was soft under my bare feet as I climbed to double golden doors set in the mist at the top of three steps of clear quartz crystal. Under the steps was a brown, blurred movement.

I went up the crystal steps to the golden doors and gently pushed them open. Before me was a beautiful meadow with yellow butterflies flying among the flowers. I breathed deeply of the perfumed air.

At my right was a pond with a tiny island. A wide-spreading oak grew near the pond.

At my left was a white cottage with its door partly open. A huge pink crystal towered beyond a flower garden. Past the crystal huddled a small wood, then a calm, blue lake.

My long dress had the meadow pattern with yellow butterflies flying from flower to flower. "How can that be?" I wondered.

"I know," said a voice from the white globe of light bobbing beside me. "Who are you?" I asked.

"Call me Inner Voice. I'm the voice inside your head."

"Is there a meaning when butterflies can fly on my dress?"

Inner Voice answered, "There is a meaning to everything, both here and in the Awake World. If you were a man, you would be wearing something that had meaning for you."

The globe of light expanded until I was standing inside it. Its inner surface was a mirror. So here I was, inside a globe of light talking with Inner Voice from inside my head.

Suddenly my mirror image blurred. "Why?" I asked.

"Your happy thoughts have been clouded by worried or fearful thoughts from the Awake World," came the answer.

"I have many fearful thoughts," I told Inner Voice. "I can't help it."

Inner Voice told me, "You can clear the energies of fearful thoughts. First, imagine a star with shimmering rays of the hues of love. "

That was easy.

"Now watch the mirror and imagine sparkles of love flowing from the star down into you."

A stream of sparkles came down and swirled inside me. How happy I felt!

When the sparkles were gone, the mirror image was clear. And I still felt happy. Amazing.

"You can be happy wherever you are," Inner Voice told me. "Look."

My reflection showed me with short black hair, wearing a long, red dress. As I felt my hair, the mirror image felt her hair. My skin was a soft yellow like hers. Unusual but pretty music played.

"Look to your right," said Inner Voice.

I turned. Now I was wearing colorful material draped around me. My skin was very dark and as I felt my hair, my reflection felt its crinkly, black hair. My feet wanted to dance to the wonderful drum beats but before I could dance a step, my image changed again.

I had golden brown skin and dark brown hair. I wore a brief top and a grass skirt with a red flower in my hair. Beautiful happy music played and ocean waves whooshed onto the beach.

Next, I had an elegant feather in my long, black hair. My leather dress had beaded designs. Drums throbbed and flute notes rose and fell.

Suddenly, all the drums boomed at once and I was in the meadow wearing my dress with fluttering yellow butterflies. The globe of light bobbed beside me.

Inner Voice asked how I felt each time I was a different person.

"I looked like different people of the world and heard their music."

"Think," said Inner Voice. "How did you <u>feel</u> when you were each person?"

"I felt like myself. And I felt happy," I answered.

"That's right," Inner Voice said, "People everywhere are happy to be themselves. They enjoy their own music and their own ways."

My Dream Scene shimmered. "Your dream is ending," said Inner Voice. "It's time to go back."

"Thanks," I called to her as I ran across the meadow, through shimmering golden doors and down the crystal steps.

As I slipped into the Awake World I thought, "Maybe next time I'll find the red-tailed hawk."

CHAPTER 3

A Red Dream

The hawk was not in sight as I climbed the grassy hill. Blurred shapes still moved under the crystal steps.

I pushed open the golden doors and saw the cottage and garden. A narrow waterfall tumbled down the small mountain into the pond, but no hawk.

My dress had filmy red tiers fluttering in the breeze. "This must be a red dream," I said.

A plant with lacy leaves popped out of the grass and quickly grew high as my shoulder with a large, red flower at the end.

The petals dropped to reveal a red, heart-shaped berry. The fruit fell into my hand, and I popped it in my mouth.

That berry melted into the most delicious juice I'd ever tasted. I swallowed and the wonderful flavor flowed through me into my fingertips, my eyes, all of me. 

Another plant grew and others beyond that. I went from one plant to the next enjoying the red fruit.

The last plant was beside a stream from the pond. As I ate that berry a chime sounded, and a red light flashed over the middle of the stream. The light dropped into the water and flashed below the surface as if to say, "Come on in."

Why not? I stepped into the water. Silky sand squeezed up through my toes. In midstream as I neared the flashing light, I stepped over the edge of a drop-off.

I floated down, light as a feather, until my feet touched the sandy bottom. Amazing! I was breathing water as though it were air. As far as I could see there were no fish, no weeds, just me.

Another chime and the light moved upstream. I followed. The water flowed through me and I soon felt crystal clear. What a wonderful red dream this was!

I sat on the sandy stream bed to think about the meaning of red. Hmmm.

Red was strawberries, apples, roses, rainbows, sunsets and flowers. There were shades of red from light pink to dark red but exactly what was red itself?

The red light winked, waiting for my answer.

Red was what I was feeling – totally happy, as though I could never stop smiling. I decided that red was love.

Whatever the shade of red, it means "I am love," with as many kinds of love as there are shades of red. "The red berries are a flavor of love," I exclaimed.

The red light shot out sparkling rays of pink light in agreement.

Points of color poked out of the sand. I dug up crystals of many colors. If only I could take them with me to the Awake World.

A rumbling sounded from upstream. Swirling bubbles appeared, coming closer. I dropped the crystals as bubbles swirled around me. I shut my eyes and softly floated down, down.

When I opened my eyes, I was at the bottom of the grassy hill. Everything was shimmering. My red dream was ending.

"Maybe I can't keep the crystals," I said, "but my happy feeling is enough. And I will always remember the meaning of red: I am love."

I smiled as I slipped from my shimmering Dream Scene into the Awake World, remembering the red berries' flavor of love.

And I was absolutely sure I'd find the red-tailed hawk in another dream, soon.

CHAPTER 4

A Yellow Dream

I went up the hill, up the crystal steps and through the golden doors. My dress was yellow, so this was a yellow dream.

The white cottage was light yellow. I walked past sunny nasturtiums to the open door.

"Is anybody home?" I called. No answer. "Of course," I said. "This is my dream, so the cottage is mine, too." I went inside.

The single room was bright and airy with the furniture facing a long blank wall. Near the door was an oak rocking chair with soft cushions, then a brass bed with a fluffy, white bedspread and many pillows.

Past the bed was a U-shaped desk with arms at the ends, like arms ready to give a big oaken hug. Chairs lined the outer sides of the arms with one behind the desk.

A tall wooden frame beyond the desk looked like a full-length mirror, without the mirror.

I tried the rocking chair. It clicked like a metronome, and I hummed in time. The bed looked so comfortable I might fall asleep if I lay down. I chuckled at the idea of falling asleep in a dream.

I sat at the desk. On it were a clock, a forever calendar, a pitcher, a glass, pens and other office things.

Looking at the pitcher, I said, "I'm thirsty." The pitcher filled with water. When I lifted the glass to drink, an empty glass appeared on the desk. I set the glass of water down and picked up the empty one. A third empty glass appeared.

"I get it," I said, "a glass of water for each of my friends." I drank my water and stacked the glasses into a single glass again.

A desk drawer held a pile of folders, the top one labeled "Dreams." I lay it open on the desk.

A sheet of paper was titled, "Rules for the Dreamer." Rules? I began reading:

Rules for the Dreamer

Rule One – *The dreamer should have awareness of the dream.*

> I knew this was a yellow dream but what did 'awareness of the dream' mean?

Rule Two – *Notice everything you see and hear in a dream.*

> Dreams have so many details. Maybe I just was supposed to try.

Rule Three – *Learn the lessons a dream teaches.*

Lessons? I thought dreams were for fun, not lessons.

Rule Four – *Learn to control the action of the dream.*

"Ridiculous!" I stuffed the folder back. "Who wrote those rules anyway? My yellow dream is dreaming itself and that's that."

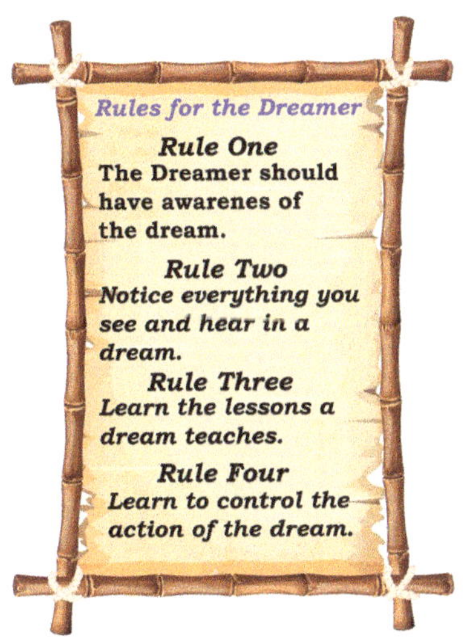

A mist formed in the wooden frame. A woman wearing a long yellow robe stepped from the frame into the room. Her silvery-white hair reached the hem of her robe.

She sat at the end of one of the desk arms, fingering her honey-colored pendant. "I came to tell you what you can learn in this room," she said. "Learn?" I echoed. "This is just a dream."

"Just a dream? You read the *Rules for the Dreamer,* so you know dreams have a purpose. Even when you come here to rest, you can learn something. If you have a problem, you will find an information folder on it in the desk."

She ignored my shrug. "You can set the clock and calendar for any time period. To talk to someone from the past, you invite them to come through the time portal as I just did."

There were eight chairs at the desk extensions. I asked if eight people can come at one time. She answered. "If you invite them, they will come. The better you know them, the more you will learn."

I told her about the rocking chair and the songs that came to my mind. Her response was, "There is music in every living thing." "Does the bed do something special, too?" I asked.

She stood. "That's for you to discover." She walked to the wooden frame and disappeared through it. I had forgotten to ask her name.

I climbed on the bed and leaned against the pillows facing the blank wall. Maybe this was a game.

"All right, a game," I said. "Pretend I am at a beach." Instantly, the wall disappeared revealing a sandy beach with the sea extending to the horizon. Sea gulls glided past, and waves flowed onto the sand.

Suddenly everything shimmered. My yellow dream was ending. I would have to enjoy the beach another time.

As I slipped into the Awake World, I heard the hawk call in the distance. Already I was eager for my next dream...and the hawk. I had to find the hawk.

CHAPTER 5

An Orange Dream

I climbed the grassy hill and stopped at the crystal steps. Those blurred, brown shapes under them looked like different kinds of chocolate melting together.

I pushed open the golden doors. My dress was orange. Just ahead of me was a large orange ball.

As I walked toward the ball it moved away. I stopped and it stopped. I took a few steps, and the ball moved ahead. What fun!

I ran and it rolled to the bottom of the wide-spreading oak near the pond. I went past the tree and sat near the pond. Then slowly I moved back, focusing on the pond. Little fish swam in the shallow water – red fish, white fish, yellow fish and blue fish.

As a blue fish and a yellow fish crossed paths, they became green. A white fish and a red one crossed paths and became pink.

While watching the fish color-blending, I inched back toward the orange ball. I saw branches overhead and gave a backward push, turning to grab the ball.

In an explosion of orange light, I tumbled down a slope into a small cave. The orange ball pulsed brightly as a rhythmic drumbeat sounded. As the drum beat vibrated through me, I danced clockwise to the rhythm.

The drum stopped and the orange ball rolled into a tunnel opening. I followed, because the only light came from the ball moving down the tunnel.

The tunnel was like a blood vessel winding through the body of the earth and the sphere seemed like a big orange corpuscle.

At the tunnel's end, I found myself in a small space under a skylight. A golden square showed through. I was under the crystal steps looking up at the golden doors!

The orange ball melted into the wall of earth and blurry brown shapes came out of the wall. The drum beat resumed, and the blurry shapes swayed in time with the beat.

"Who are you?" I asked the shapes.

One of them answered, "We are life energy beings who help everything on earth that grows. We carry the heartbeat of earth to all things on the earth."

The earth was alive with a heartbeat and life energy beings. "Are you part of my dream," I asked, "or are you something real that has come into my dream?"

"We have existed forever in the mind of the Creator of all things, just as all dreams and creations have always been," was the answer.

This was hard to understand. I asked, "If all creations exist in the mind of the Creator as you said, then are all things part of everything else? Is that possible?" The reply: "It is not only possible, it IS so."

I thought of everything I'd ever seen from a grain of sand to stars, from food I ate to the dream I was dreaming. If they all were part of everything everywhere, was I one with the earth and even these earth energies?

I shook my head. "How can that be?"

The reply: "It IS what it is. Accept your oneness with all things or be isolated from all things. The choice is yours."

"What is the orange ball of light?" I asked.

"It's the energy of life that is within everything that exists."
"Even me?" I questioned.

"You exist, therefore that energy is within your being."

I remembered the hawk. "If I am one with the hawk, why can't I find it?"

The answer, "When the hawk wants to be found, you will find it. Until then, be satisfied that the hawk let you see it in your first dream."

"How do I get out of here?" I asked, pointing to the crystal steps overhead. Their answer came with a gentle but strong lifting as the earth beings carried me upward. The crystal allowed me to float through it.

I stood beside the crystal steps and waved to the earth beings. "Thanks for what you do for us all," I said.

My dream shimmered to an end. I was glad that the energy of my orange dream was part of me, even in the Awake World.

As I slipped into the Awake World, I said, "If I am one with everything I think about, I will try to think about good things."

I opened my eyes and smiled. "I can find a lot of good things to think about in the Awake World. That will be easy – I think."

CHAPTER 6

A Green Dream

The hawk wasn't anywhere. I went up the crystal steps and pushed open the golden doors.

An opening in the grassy meadow revealed steps of delicate green crystal.

I called down, "Is anybody there?" The only sound was the waterfall splashing behind me. The steps were cool under my bare feet as I started down.

The sides of the steps were very wide, and each step curved even wider. At the bottom, I saw a green glint in the grass. On a silver cord was a round medallion of the same crystal as the steps. I hung it around my neck.

I turned to compare the medallion with the steps, but the steps were gone. "How will I get back?" I said out loud.

"A step at a time," came a voice from behind me. A man stood between two tall columns of clear quartz. He wore a white Grecian-style garment and a green medallion exactly like mine.

"Who are you?" I asked. "You weren't here a minute ago."

"Call me Croesus if you like," he said. "I came from my dream just as you came from yours."

"Why are you dressed like that?" I asked.

"Why are you dressed as you are?" was his response. I looked down at my white, Grecian gown.

He smiled. "I said you may call me Croesus. I didn't say that's who I am."

He placed his hands on the columns. Spots of light moved up and down the columns then burst into rainbow colors like fireworks. He took his hands away and the columns were clear again.

Gesturing toward his medallion, I asked, "What is the green?"

"It's chrysolite, a stone of intent and healing. My intent is that you reach into yourself to discover your own intent, your strength."

When I didn't respond, he said, "It can help heal emotional pain, if you so intend."

"What were those lights in the columns," I asked defiantly. Croesus laughed. "A way to get your attention."

"I don't care what your intent is. I want to go back to my own Dream Scene," I said.

"It isn't enough to want to go back. You need a strong intent to go back." He gestured toward the columns. "Place your hands on them the way I did."

I jumped back and shouted, "I will not!" What kind of trick was this?

He silently waited.

Doing nothing wouldn't get me back so I put my hands on the columns. "Now <u>feel</u> a strong intent to go back," he said.

I thought about finding the green steps so I could go back. "It didn't work," I said.

"You need to <u>feel</u> your intent. Try harder."

Irritation niggled at my mind. "I want to go back," I declared, a bit louder than necessary. Again, and again. Suddenly, bubbles of light rose up the columns.

Croesus laughed. "You've got the idea," he said.

I dropped my hands. "Don't laugh. And how will bubbles get me back?"

"The bubbles, as you call them, show the strength of your intent. Wishing isn't enough. Deeply feel and see yourself back in the meadow. Make going back as real as being here. That's the secret."

I stared him down. "I can't get back because the stairs are gone."

Croesus reached over and touched my green chrysolite medallion. "This is your stairs." He touched his own medallion. "This is my stairs. That's how I came, just as you did."

I looked at my medallion. "This is the stairs?"

"If you so intend," was his reply.

"How can a medallion turn back into stairs?" I asked.

Croesus said, "By strongly feeling your intent as if you already were back.

Be your intent and feel the chrysolite stairs under your feet. You can do it."

I took the medallion from my neck and laid it on the grass. "I don't want the medallion to be around my neck when it turns into the steps."

Croesus' laugh was almost a shout. "You've got the idea!"

Placing my hands on the columns, I took a deep breath and willed the chrysolite stairs back.

Bubbles of light raced up and down the columns. "Intensify the intent," I told myself over and over.

An explosion of light rose up the columns, and in an instant, I was standing at the top of the green chrysolite stairs.

I wondered if Croesus used his medallion to return to his Dream Scene. It didn't matter. I was back.

My thoughts were full of Croesus and chrysolite, feelings and intent. As I walked toward the golden doors, everything began to shimmer.

The red-tailed hawk had not appeared in this dream, but I knew I'd see it in a future dream because that was my intent.

CHAPTER 7

A Pink Dream

I sat at the foot of the grassy hill. My day had been heart-heavy, and my sadness was in a heavy bundle on my back. The grassy hill shimmered.

I closed my eyes, ready to wake up without going to my Dream Scene. A sudden, sharp call sent electricity down my arms and legs.

The red-tailed hawk! I jumped up expecting to see it circling above but it was nowhere in sight.

My sorrow-bundle slid off my back onto the grass. I hurried to open the golden doors. The tall, pink crystal was glowing, so I went there.

When I touched the crystal, my hands sank into it. I pushed my hands further in, then followed with my whole body into a large, pink room. Clusters of pink quartz crystals decorated the walls.

A rosy glow formed and from it stepped a woman wearing a long pink robe, her white hair reaching the hem of her robe. Hanging from her braided silver belt was a small pouch. She was in my yellow dream!

"What's your name?" I asked.

She smiled. "I am Ara." Then, "Would you like to sit?" I looked around the empty room. "Sit where?"

"Anywhere you create something for sitting," she answered. "I can't do that."

Ara gestured toward the pink quartz clusters. "You created these and everything else in your Dream Scene."

Where in the Awake World would I have seen the things in my Dream Scene? The flowery meadow was like a field on my grandparents' farm. The rose garden with marble benches and fountain was like a birthday card picture.

This pink crystal was a giant version of one in my nightstand drawer.

I asked, "Is everything in by Dream Scene from the Awake World?"

"Yes," she said. "Do you know how they came to your Dream Scene?" I didn't know.

"You brought them with you," said Ara. "Everything you see in the Awake World is part of you both there and here. So, remember something for sitting." I thought of a velvety, white chair I had seen at a furniture store. At that moment, that same chair was behind me. "How did that happen?" I asked.

Ara answered, "Your thoughts create your personal world. This happens quickly in a Dream Scene."

I thought of a pink chair behind Ara. Instantly, there it was. We sat.

I looked at the crystal clusters on the walls. Where had I seen them before? As if reading my mind Ara said, " Crystals are energy and these crystal clusters are the energy of your thoughts."

She continued, "When you plan a gift for instance, your thoughts cluster around ideas. Those thoughts crystallize into lovely arrangements like these." So many crystal clusters. I grinned. "I must spend a lot of time thinking."

Ara smiled. "Everyone does. You also take ideas from here to the Awake World. Look for treasures in both the Awake World and your Dream Scene." Quickly I said, "I don't notice details."

Ara unfastened the pouch from her belt. "Hold out your hands."

I cupped my hands. From the pouch she took a heart of clear blue quartz and one of pink quartz. She dropped them into my hands. "Hold the hearts against your throat."

I did. Startled, I dropped my hands and stared. They were empty.

Ara said, "My gift to you with these hearts is that you will see and speak with the clarity of the blue quartz and with the love of the pink quartz."

"But I have no gift for you," I said.

"Your gift to me is to use my gift to you." "I will, Ara," I said softly. "Thank you."

"And I thank you," she said. The rosy glow formed again. With a wave Ara stepped into it and was gone. The chairs were gone, too.

I went back through the pink quartz wall to the meadow. I tried to remember where in the Awake World I'd seen the mountain and the waterfall...maybe in Colorado.

My Dream Scene began to shimmer. I put my hands on my throat and said, "I want to see all things and people with clarity and love the way Ara told me."

Then I wondered, where did Ara come from? Maybe I wasn't supposed to know, just as the man who called himself Croesus kept his real identity a secret.

"Be satisfied," I told myself. "This was a good pink dream."

I walked through the shimmering golden doors and down the grassy hill. My sorrow-bundle still lay at the foot of the hill.

"That's one thing I refuse to take to the Awake World," I said and in a wink it disappeared.

Yes, this was a good pink dream.

CHAPTER 8

A Light Dream

"Follow your intuition, your inner voice," I thought as I climbed the hill. I read that in a book somewhere.

I went through the golden doors and felt drawn to the waterfall. Soon I was under it with the cleansing waters flowing through me.

A glint caught my eye. It was the robe of a man by the garden fountain. My dress was shiny, too. I went to the garden.

Before I could speak, the man said, "Greetings. I am Phlebas." "You said your name was Croesus. Remember?" I told him.

He laughed. "And do you remember I said you could call me Croesus, but didn't say that was my name?"

I sat on a marble bench and breathed in the fragrance of roses.

He said, "You are going to use your inner sight to see colors your physical eyes can't see. See yourself in a sphere of white light that flows through you."

That's like the waterfall, I thought. I not only saw the sphere of white light around me, I felt it.

"White light protects and strengthens," Phlebas explained. "The light is the divine essence in the spaces between and within the atoms of your being." He paused. "Change to green light."

Swirls of electric green light flowed around and through me. Suddenly, I cried out, "I can't feel my stomach or legs."

Phlebas said, "Those areas have blockages you created with negative energy of fear or anger."

"How did I do that?" I asked.

Phlebas replied, "You've been in a situation that you say you 'can't stomach' but you don't change it or 'walk away' from it."

"How does that make my legs and stomach numb?"

He answered. "Fear and indecision block energies from freely moving. You need to remove the blockage."

He continued. "Concentrate on green light going to your stomach and legs. Apologize to the numb areas and ask their forgiveness for negative thoughts."

"Apologize to my body?" I asked. Phlebas waited.

Finally, I made an apology of sorts and imaged green light going into my stomach and legs. Moving light was tricky. Other thoughts kept interfering. I tried many times before succeeding.

Phlebas said, "Now you know how green light can help heal a blocked area." He smiled. "It's even better if you don't think negative thoughts."

Then he told me to focus on blue light. Green gave way to electric blue.

He continued. "Blue strengthens your will and intent. Wrap that blue light around you and intensify your desire for will power to create and reach goals."

I visualized blue light, then said I'd like to know how to use all colors. A golden light filled my head, spilled out of the top and flowed around me. "Wow! That happened when I wanted to learn about all colors!"

Phlebas said, "When you seek knowledge, focus on yellow. It helps draw answers to you. Other seekers of knowledge will be drawn to you, too."

Yellow was a wonderful, joyous color. I was so excited I could hardly sit still.

The yellow deepened and became clear orange.

"Orange," Phlebas explained, "is a blend of yellow mental energy and red physical energy. Finding ways to use light enriches our lives."

"If everyone used light this way," I said, "they could be happy, too."

Pink light flooded my inner vision as I felt love for everyone. I mentally hugged the world and everyone in it. I remembered that the meaning of red was love and pink was one of the hues of love.

Phlebas confirmed that pink light was, indeed, an expression of love and told me to use and send it often.

"Phlebas, what is the violet light I sometimes see when my eyes are shut?" "You mean this?" he asked. Around me glowed rosy-violet light and I felt a surge of peace and harmony.

I nodded.

"In rosy-violet light are the pink of love and the violet of higher spirituality," Phlebas said. "Use violet light to send harmony and peace to everyone in the world. The need is great."

He added, "Visualizing a sphere of light around people is a loving gift. Any color is a gift, but white light contains all the colors."

I remembered the author who said in his book, "Follow your inner voice." I closed my eyes and popped white light around him with my thanks.

At a sharp call from the hawk, I opened my eyes and found myself at the foot of the shimmering hill. High above circled the hawk. I popped white light around the hawk. "A gift, my friend."

Remembering what Phlebas said about negative thoughts, again I apologized to myself for my many 'you're-never-good-enough' thoughts about myself.

Suddenly, I was in a sphere of bright golden-white light that glinted with tiny sparks of color. I'd given myself a gift!

"Thank you," I told myself as I slipped into the Awake World.

An Angry Dream

My anger grew as I ran up the grassy hill. Just wait until I gave Phlebas a piece of my mind for causing my bad experience that day.

I ignored the earth spirits and pushed hard on the golden doors, eager to vent my anger at Phlebas in the garden. I stopped.

Fog hid my Dream Scene except for the cottage, which was bright yellow. The door was open.

Rules for the Dreamer said I create my Dream Scene, but I definitely had not created that fog.

"What choice do I have?" I muttered and entered the cottage.

Phlebas sat at one of the long arms of the desk. "I've been waiting for you."

My anger flared. "You caused me enough trouble today without fogging up my Dream Scene!"

"The fog was created from your own fuzzy thinking" he said. "It was difficult to keep the cottage free of fog so you could find me."

I plunged into my story. "Putting white light around people doesn't work. It backfired when I tried it today!"

I told him how I was behind a woman at the grocery checkout. She had held up the line digging for car keys.

"I popped white light around her like you said, to help her think better." Phlebas nodded approval. "That was the right thing to do."

I glared accusingly at him. "Well, she turned and gave me a hateful look, just because I put the light around her."

Phlebas asked, "And that's what you think happened?"

"Of course, that's what happened. I was there, you weren't," I snapped. "Sometimes we don't see the whole picture," Phlebas said. He led me to the middle of the room facing the blank wall and said, "Look."

The wall faded away and there was the grocery store scene. Phlebas and I were behind the counter, facing the young woman digging for her keys.

I saw myself in line behind her. She was biting her lower lip. "She is trying not to cry," said Phlebas.

At that moment the woman was surrounded by white light. 'That was me popping the light around her," I said. "Then she gave me that angry look." "Listen," said Phlebas. "You will hear her thoughts."

The woman's heart area was soft pink. "Oh, Dad, why did you die? I love you so much. It's not fair!"

That was the moment she turned toward me showing her anguish and grief.

I was speechless. She hadn't been angry at me after all.

"The pink light reflected her love for her father," explained Phlebas.

The woman found her keys and we watched her take the groceries to her car. She sat behind the wheel and sobbed. "I miss you, Dad."

I was ashamed of my anger with her and with Phlebas. My assumptions had been wrong about both of them.

"But Phlebas, how was I to know?"

He smiled. "In the Awake World, you can't see behind the masks that people wear to know what they are feeling. You, too, wear masks that hide your thoughts and feelings.

"It's as foolish to be upset when you don't see behind others' masks," he continued, "as it is to be upset when others can't understand your real feelings behind your mask.

He said, "You gave the young woman a gift of light, a kind gesture, yet you were sorry you gave it when you thought her glance at you was hateful. What does that teach you?"

'I'm sorry I got angry with her. I didn't understand her problem." "Good," Phlebas responded, "but what does that teach you?"

I paused, then, "We should send light to others without expectations?" "Exactly," he said. "I knew the answer was in you. It was just a matter of unfogging your judgment."

I had a question. "You said the fog in my Dream Scene was of my own making. How did I do that without knowing what I was doing?"

Phlebas answered with a question. "When you come to your Dream Scene, how do you create an experience you never had before?"

It wasn't fair of him to answer with a question, but I hadn't been fair to vent my anger at him. "Phlebas, I'm sorry I was upset with you," I said.

"Apology accepted," he replied, "but your anger didn't upset me. I just sent you light. It's a privilege to send light, any color, to everything and everybody."

The cottage room began to shimmer. My dream was ending. "Thanks, Phlebas. This was a wonderful dream." I popped pink light around him and ran out the door.

The fog was gone. My Dream Scene shimmered. I wondered about my unanswered question to Phlebas then remembered what Ara said: "I create my Dream Scene experiences with whatever I take with me from the Awake World." Wow!

Suddenly I was surrounded by white light. I turned to see Phlebas waving at me by the golden doors.

I drifted into the Awake World cradled in Phlebas' gift of white light.

CHAPTER 10

A Feelings Dream

At the bottom of the grassy hill an open, white bag floated a few inches off the grass. On it was written: "Deposit Worries Here."

I closed my eyes and imaged my problems and worries drifting out the top of my head and dropping into the bag.

When I opened my eyes, the bag was tied shut and rested heavily on the grass.

I felt light as air as I ran up the hill, waved to the earth beings under the crystal steps and went through the golden doors.

I felt oddly empty without my worries. "I'm not my worries," I reminded myself, "but I don't know what I want to do."

Jokingly I said, "If I don't know what I want, maybe I don't even know who I am."

The cottage door opened, and Ara came out. Remembering her gift of the blue and pink quartz hearts I touched my throat. Had I used them correctly?

"Don't worry about that," Ara said. "Remember, you left your worries behind." We both laughed and she added, "Do you really want to know who you are?"

I nodded. My dress was of the same sparkly material as her robe.

Ara assured me, "There is more to who you are than what you see. Come." We went inside. She gestured toward the blank wall which now was a mirror.

"Is your reflection who you think you are?" she asked.

It looked like me.

"Observe your feelings," Ara said. 'What if you had no arms?"

I gasped. My arms were gone, both on my body and in the mirror. "And if you had no body?"

Now my head was floating in the air. "What's going on?"

Ara calmly said, "Observe your feelings about the illusion you are seeing." It was weird. I was just a floating head yet I felt the same as before.

"Now watch," she said. In a blink, my head was gone.

Even without a body, I gasped again. I saw Ara in the mirror, but I had disappeared. "How can I see when I have no body or head?"

Ara laughed. "You are not your body, remember? Look closely."

I saw a small spot of intense white light. "Is that all I am? A bit of light?"

"Is that all you are?" Ara echoed. "Think what a marvelous being you are right now. You think, you feel, you move about. There is even more to who you are. Come outside."

I followed her out of the cottage and across the meadow, amazed to be moving without a body. She stopped beside the oak tree near the pond.

"This tree has feelings, too," Ara said. "Go into the tree and you will understand."

"I can't go inside a tree."

Ara reminded me, "You are not your body. Right now, you are who you really are, and you can go into the tree as a visitor and friend."

I went up to the tree's rough bark, then moved forward a little more and found myself inside the tree. If I had eyes, they would have been wide open.

From inside the tree, I could see everything outside. I felt the wonderful aliveness of the tree and its strength, from the powerful roots to its leafy branches. It hummed a beautiful melody.

"Isn't the tree wonderful?" Ara said. "Now visit the pond."

As soon as I thought of it, I was in the water of the pond. Liquid love! I flowed like water, even through the rainbow of fish. I flowed into pebbles and grass, into flowers and butterflies. I was an exhilarating dance of love. Everywhere love.

"It's time to go." Ara interrupted.

"I wish I could do this in the Awake World, too." I told her.

"You are not your body," Ara said. 'Who you are right now can visit all things in this way, in your Dream Scene or the Awake World."

"Awake bodies can't go inside trees or butterflies," I said.

"Go back to your question; Who am I?" Ara suggested. "Right now, without your physical body, who are you?"

All I was sure of was that I wanted to feel this way forever.

She prompted, "You are what you feel."

If I had a body, it would have shivered with delight. "Right now, I'm feeling love and joy, total happiness."

"And that's who you really are, love and joy," said Ara. "The tree is love. So is everything that exists and you are one with all of them. In the Awake World you let worry and care come into your feelings until you forget who you truly are."

"Everybody has worries," I said. 'That's part of life."

Her response was, "Knowing and accepting one's responsibilities is different from endlessly churning over worries. Fretting doesn't solve problems."

She smiled. "Who you are right now is who you really are."

"Right now, I am love and joy," I said. My Dream Scene shimmered, and in an instant, I was in my dream body at the bottom of the grassy hill, standing by the big, lumpy bag of my worries and cares.

"You aren't part of me," I told the bag of worries. The bag disappeared. "Ara was right" I said. "I am neither my Awake nor my Dream body. I'm just love and joy."

With a happy smile, love and joy slipped out of my Dream Scene and into the Awake World.

CHAPTER 11

An In-My-Heart Dream

I waved to the earth beings under the crystal steps and pushed open the golden doors.

A beam of light streamed onto the meadow grass. I walked toward it, and I stepped into the beam. It gently urged me toward the garden.

I walked to the garden and the light came with me. I reached the garden fountain, and the light vanished.

Fragrance of roses scented the air. I sat on a marble bench. "If only everyone could feel as happy as I do right now," I said.

"That's a good wish," said a voice behind me.

It was a woman in a white robe. She was taller than Ara. Her frizzy yellow hair was styled in pouts at the sides of her head. "I am ZsuZsu," she said. "Would you like to make your wish come true?"

"Impossible," I told her. "I can't change the whole world." She sat beside me and asked, "Would you like to try?"

I nodded.

"Good," she said. "Relax and feel the energy flow out of your heart to create a small Earth floating in front of you."

I took a deep breath and let it out in a sigh, relaxing completely. I imaged a globe of Earth the size of a small orange floating in front of me.

"Now picture your galaxy," said ZsuZsu.

Remembering pictures of the Milky Way Galaxy, I focused on a place beside my little Earth and soon a transparent globe with the planets and billions of stars inside it floated beside the Earth. So beautiful.

Then ZsuZsu said, "Now visualize brilliant white light around each globe penetrating to the center of each and energizing every atom."

I followed her suggestion and saw the two globes inside spheres of white light.

ZsuZsu rested a finger on her cheek. "Very good," she said. "The light is touching everyone and everything on Earth and throughout the galaxy. You are actually sending the light vibration to them. Now use pink light the same way."

I tingled with the fun of creating and as I imaged the globes surrounded by electric pink light I said, "Here is love for all of you."

"Now," ZsuZsu said, "see both spheres of light encircled with the violet light of harmony, and white light round the violet."

When I did that, ZsuZsu smiled. "Now picture your heart inside its own sphere of violet and white light." That was easy.

"Next, take a deep breath and image the Earth globe and the galaxy globe moving into your heart light."

I took a deep breath, and in a flash the two globes were in my heart. "They are part of me now, right?"

"Yes," ZsuZsu confirmed. "They always have been but now you are aware of it. You make your wish for peace and happiness in the world a reality by keeping the light around them in your heart."

"ZsuZsu" I asked, "are we all one in the light, no matter what color light I use?" There was no answer. ZsuZsu was gone. The beam of light again was at the edge of the garden.

I thought about the galaxy and the earth in my heart, with billions of people surrounded by the light. What a happy thought! When I stepped into the beam, it shimmered, and I found myself at the bottom of the shimmering hill.

When I opened my eyes in the Awake World, I knew for always I would keep the Earth and the galaxy glowing in my heart like beautiful cosmic jewels.

I knew I could send them love and light any time with just a thought and nobody will know that I am smiling because I feel so wonderful...in my heart.

CHAPTER 12

A Fear Dream

My day had been a disaster and now my dream was starting out wrong. The grassy hill and the golden doors were blurry. My fears in the Awake World had come with me to my Dream Scene.

In the meadow no butterflies flew among the flowers. The stream and waterfall were silent. My Dream Scene seemed frozen.

A lounge chair was down by the pond. The island had no tree. I sat on the lounge and closed my eyes. With all my problems in the Awake World, why worry about that tree?

I opened my eyes to be sure I was still in my Dream Scene. I was, but now a large glass tree stood in the middle of the island. Green glass leaves tinkled on sturdy glass branches.

"How did that tree get there?" I wondered out loud.

"I came because you needed me," said a vibrant voice from the tree. "How could I need you when I didn't know you existed?" I responded.

"I'm a fear-eating tree," said the tree. "I felt your fears and lured you here with the lounge. When you closed your eyes, I rooted myself where you would see me."

"You can't eat fear." I stared at the tree. "Fear is just a feeling and you don't have a mouth."

Glass leaves clinked as the tree laughed. "Tell me what your fear looks like," it said.

I answered. "Fear is invisible."

"Use your imagination," the tree persisted. "Give fear a shape and color."

As I thought about my fears, pressure on my lungs felt like a crushing black rock leaving no room for a full breath. Gray nausea in my abdomen rose into my throat. I blinked away tears.

"Now that you have imaged your fear," said the tree, "I can see it and will take it from you, but first you must want to get rid of it."

"Fear is scary. Why would I want to keep it?" I asked.

The glass tree responded, 'What's important is: How hard are you willing to try to get rid of your fear? I can take it only if you give it to me. Nothing will change unless you change."

"I don't understand," I said.

"How often has something you feared happened exactly as you imagined?" asked the tree.

"Hardly ever," I answered, "but things still happened."

The tree suggested an experiment to see if losing my fear would help change circumstances. This was a dream, so why not?

"What do I have to do?" I asked.

"Come and place your hands on my trunk."

I waded into the pond then stepped onto the island. When I put my hands on the tree trunk they tingled. "Now what?"

"Say to your fear, 'You may leave,' and relax your emotional grip on it. Allow bits of fear to break off and flow down your arms into your hands so I can take it from you."

"You may leave now," I said to the black rock in my chest and the gray nausea. Nothing happened. I repeated it until I felt bits of gray nausea and black fear break off and move down my arms into my hands.

"Look at that!" I exclaimed as the bits appeared inside the glass tree trunk then shredded apart and disappeared. More bits of fear disappeared into the tree, and I did feel better. Soon no gray nausea or black fear remained inside me.

"Now that the fear is removed, that space must be filled so the fear can't come back. Put your arms around my trunk."

I hugged the tree and pressed my cheek against it. A cheerful contentment flowed through me.

The tree explained. "When fear is removed, the space must be filled with love."

Just now, I gave you energies of love. You can do that for yourself, too."

"Thank you!" I told the fear-eating tree, marveling at the experience.

"You aren't finished," informed the tree. "You need to know how to remove fear yourself. Relax on the lounge chair."

I waded through the pond to the lounge chair and leaned into its softness. "Close your eyes and image white light all around you," instructed the tree. I visualized white light around me and the chair.

The tree continued. "Breathe white light into your whole body. See white light fill every part of you."

After a few breaths I saw white light coming into me from head to toe. "Now, each time you exhale image the light taking bits of fear from you and flowing with it out the bottoms of your feet into the Earth where the fear dissolves and disappears."

Soon I was breathing in light and breathing out fear. Awesome!

The tree gave the next step. "As you exhale, let your muscles go soft and limp, totally relaxed. First focus only on relaxing your face muscles, then your arms and so on. 'In with the light and out with the fear' until all groups of muscles experience the feeling of releasing fear. Soon you will be able to exhale fear from your entire body at the same time."

I closed my eyes. It wasn't easy at first but with the tree's encouragement to "practice, practice, practice," relaxing became like melting into the lounge chair.

I opened my eyes to thank the fear-eating tree and found myself at the bottom of the shimmering grassy hill. The double golden doors shimmered. My dream was ending.

I slipped into the Awake World with a smile, happy to know the fear-eating tree would always be there if I needed it – just like a very special friend.

CHAPTER 13

A Stag Dream

The red-tailed hawk wasn't in sight as I went up the crystal steps.

I pushed open the golden doors and scanned my Dream Scene from the edge of the meadow. Butterflies flew up. "Hello, to you, too," I said.

There was no special sign or color, so I headed for the wide-spreading oak by the pond and leaned against the tree.

"This is my dream, and I really want to see the hawk so why doesn't it show up?" I grumbled.

A soft thudding came from behind the tree and a majestic stag appeared. "Why do you think you can command the hawk to come to you?"

"Deer can't talk!" I blurted.

"Everything has something to say," said the stag, "even me."

I hadn't meant to imply the stag wasn't intelligent. "I'm sorry."

The stag nodded acceptance of my apology. "You can't understand a person from another country until you learn their language. It's the same with all life."

Each nation of life has its own language – humans, animals, plants, rocks and even your hawk.”

“Do you speak only in dreams?” I asked.

“You could speak with me in the Awake World if you learned my language.” “Schools don’t teach your language.”

The stag responded, “If you know how to listen, you can learn the languages of all things. Even rocks have wisdom to share.”

"Here, maybe," I said, "but not in the Awake World." "Tell me what you know about atoms," said the stag. "What do atoms have to do with language?" I asked.

The stag replied with a question. "Do you know there is space between atoms?"

"Of course," I answered.

"What fills those spaces in the atoms of all that exists?" the stag asked. His eyes were soft and gentle.

"Phlebas said white light of divine love fills those spaces," I said.

"Right," responded the stag, "and in that light of love is life that connects everything everywhere to everything else. Through this connection, you can learn the language of all beings."

My mind whirled with questions I didn't know how to ask.

"These dreams have lessons you don't understand until you experience the adventure of the dream, right?" The stag tossed his antlers in emphasis. "Yes, but where do the dreams come from?" I asked.

"Now we are making progress," said the stag. "Your dreams come from your connection to the things around you and to things you are connected to but have yet to know."

I was excited that everything in my Dream Scene and the Awake World was connected by the light of love to everything in the farthest reaches of the universe. Countless universes! And life itself was that light of love!

The stag asked, "Where in you is the focus of that connection to all life?" I felt the stag's love for me and my love for him. I said, "My focus of connection is my heart, right?"

"Very good," said the stag. "Through your heart connection you can learn to understand the language of all others. Love and light flow in an endless stream to everything that exists, whether it is a person, a tree, a planet or even your hawk. All life is connected."

I waited for him to continue. He asked, "Do you realize that when you dream the hawk into your dream, the hawk is dreaming you into its dream?"

At that moment, the red-tailed hawk called from the mist at the top of the small mountain. My heart reached out to the hawk as it flew out of the mist and glided toward us.

It swooped down hardly ten feet in front of me. I could see the fine details of its beautiful feathers. The hawk looked at me with piercing eyes and as it passed dropped a single, rusty-red feather.

With another sharp cry the hawk flew up to the mountain and vanished into the mist.

I turned toward the stag but he, too, was gone. I picked up the feather and preened the hawk's gift.

A shimmer! I held the feather over my head and ran across the shimmering meadow to the golden doors. I felt as though I really could fly.

My dream faded and so did the feather. But the stag said everything is always connected, so the hawk's beautiful gift feather will be mine forever – in my heart.

CHAPTER 14

A Music Dream

Up the grassy hill and through the golden doors I went. The tall pink crystal was lit from within, so I headed there. Bird songs came from everywhere.

I placed my hands on the pink crystal and melted into it. The pink room had changed. On the far side was an archway to a pink tunnel. I went down the tunnel which curved toward the right.

It opened to another flowered meadow, but everything there was made of glass! Colorful glass butterflies and tiny transparent fairies flew back and forth. Soft music was everywhere.

"What's making the music?" I wondered out loud.

"All of us," said a fairy nearby. "Everything has a melody. We help plants grow when we echo their songs. Listen."

Lower, deeper chords came from the trees while lighter music came from the flowers, grass and butterflies. Fairies echoed each tone. A lovely symphony.

Rippling melodies came from a stream that flowed toward a hill. Fairies flew above the water like a musical stream.

I followed the stream into a cave where it formed a pond.

Water fairies circling over the pond sang, "Come into the water and be refreshed." They dove in and out of the water, spraying water drops which added subtle notes to the water music.

I walked into the pond. My white dress glowed under the water that reached to my shoulders in the middle of the pond. t ducked under the water which felt like silk sliding over my skin. When I popped out, the fairies' laughter trilled a melody.

I came out of the water and followed the stream as it sang its way to the far end of the cave. I stepped out into light – and nothingness. I was standing on air. I could hear the music but could see nothing, not even myself.

"What happened?" I called out. "Where am I?"

A fairy spoke. "Here we are just our life essence and our melodies blend into a great symphony."

Then I heard notes of a deeper song beneath the other melodies.

A fairy explained. "That is the song of our Earth Mother who cares for us. Melodies come from people, animals, birds and all life on Earth. Even rocks are alive with their songs."

Some notes in Earth Mother's song sounded like sad, melodic tears. "Why does she sound so sad?" I asked.

The fairy sighed. "Earth Mother has been hurt very much and she cries in pain and sorrow. Her song cries as she does." Suddenly, sharp discordant chords clashed with the other music.

"What was that?"

"That was the music of people deliberately hurting and destroying our Earth Mother and each other. Not all music is good."

Melodies came from overhead. When I asked, the fairies told me that stars and planets and everything on them sing their songs, too.

The tiny being said, "You, too, are a living melody."

"Me? Where is my melody? Are there fairies who echo my song?"

The answer was, "Your song is within you. In quiet times, go within to hear it." Then, "All people have beings to guide and help them. You can tune in to their melodies, too."

Harp chords sounded in front of me. Another melody was a harmonic humming. I saw two glowing songs in front of me.

"We are your guides, or angels if you prefer," said a deeper voice from the humming song.

"We have always been with you," said the lighter voice from the harp song.

"Others have been with you in the past and others will be with you in the future. Do you feel our song?"

I felt disoriented, surrounded only by music and nothingness.

"You are safe," said the deep voice. "Remember that you create your song from moment to moment, and by your song you are known in our dimension. Loving all things brings beauty to your song. Listen to it often and you will learn much about yourself."

The voice from the harp song said, "Each melody is part of the song of creation. When you love your own melody, you also love us and all things."

"Thank you, both of you," I told them.

I wrapped all the songs around me in a musical memory and suddenly was back at entrance to the pink crystal.

As soon as I stepped inside the pink crystal, it shimmered. I slid into the Awake World with the song of creation humming happily in my memory. "And part of that song is me," I said. Awesome!

CHAPTER 15

An Atoms Dream

My leg ached as I went up the crystal steps and pushed open the golden doors. A breeze gently rippled my silky white robe.

By the garden fountain Phlebas waved to me. He wore white Grecian attire. "You look troubled," he said.

"My left leg aches." The rose garden began to shimmer.

Phlebas touched my shoulder. "Please stay," he said. The shimmering stopped. "Before we talk about your pain, we will begin with atoms."

"I know about atoms and the space between them," I said. "And you know what is in that space?"

I said, "Like you, the stag told me that light and love in that space connect all of us with everything else."

"Schools have blackboards but I have a reflection screen." Phlebas gestured and a large mirror appeared in front of us.

"What do you see?" he asked.

I saw myself with Phlebas standing beside me. The place where my leg ached was pulsing red.

He said, "Look at your ache. Red pain has come into those spaces between atoms, but we will displace the pain with light."

I should have expected that. Phlebas had light on the brain. He could translate anything into light.

Phlebas said, "Watch the screen and image white light coming in the top of your head."

I did this and a shaft of light came into my reflection image.

Phlebas continued. "Breathe light into the spaces between every atom."

I inhaled deeply, imaging the light flowing through me like liquid. My entire reflection glowed with the light, except for that red ache.

"Very good," Phlebas said. "Breathe light into your head and when you exhale, push the light down into both legs."

As I exhaled and pushed the light into my legs, sparkles of light moved into the red, then vanished.

"It doesn't work."

Phlebas advised, "Focus on your leg with no pain. Breathe in the light and push it down into both legs as you exhale but focus your eyes on the pain-free leg. Yes, stare at that pain-free leg."

"But I can still see the red aching leg."

Phlebas smiled. "Then I will present you with flowers," he said, and a white vase of white flowers appeared in front of my aching red leg.

Again, I followed his instructions. Now it was easier to focus on my pain-free leg as I breathed in the light, then exhaled, pushing the white light into both legs. I watched my pain-free leg as it become whiter and whiter.

I didn't know how much time passed, if time even exists in a dream, but kept working until I realized, "The ache is gone in my other leg!"

Phlebas blinked away the flowers and I saw both my legs filled with white light and pain-free.

"You worked hard to replace the ache with light. That works especially well just before sleep; but always focus on the side of your body without pain. Your brain works to match what you watch."

"Thanks," I told him. "I feel so happy I could almost fly like the hawk." "Name what you are feeling," said Phlebas.

"Is it Love?"

Phlebas nodded. "Your feeling is, indeed, Love. It's also Light. You don't see the Light with your Awake eyes, but it's there."

He concluded. "Light and Love and Life are one and the same." With a grin, I said, "I never read that in any science book."

"You never will," he said.

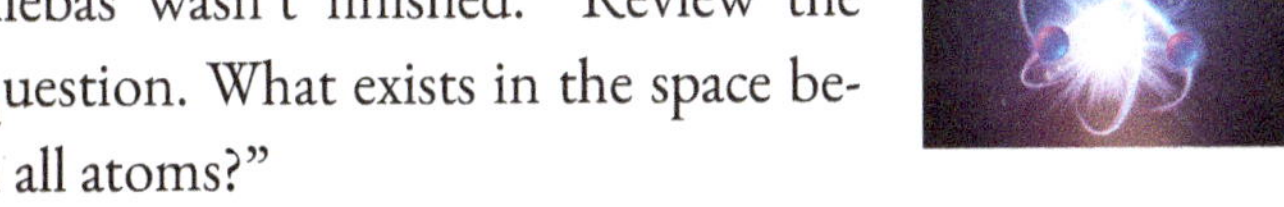

Phlebas wasn't finished. "Review the first question. What exists in the space between all atoms?"

"Three L's," I answered.

He looked at me. "Three L's?" "Right," I said, "*Love, Light* and *Life*." "Excellent!" exclaimed Phlebas.

It was like getting a gold star in an exam. I was sure he knew what I meant by the three L's, but he gave me the satisfaction of saying it myself.

Seven Directions:

"Focus on seeing the three L's in all Seven Directions." "There are only four directions," I corrected.

He smiled. "You came into your Dream Scene from the east. What is in the **east**?"

"The double golden doors."

He asked what was to the **south**. I answered, "The cottage and the big pink crystal."

"And to the **west**?" "The woods," I said.

When he asked about the **north** I answered, "The lake, pond and the mountain, and that's four directions."

"What do you see when you **look up**?" I said, "The sky."

As I expected, he next asked what I see when I **look down**. Now I understood about six directions.

"And when you **look within**, into your heart, what do you see?" I stared blankly.

"Earth, our Galaxy and everything else that exists are in your heart. The seventh direction is probably the most important one of all."

Then he asked, "What connects everything in all seven directions?" Grinning (maybe it really was a smirk), I replied, "Love, Light and Life- the three L's."

Phlebas laughed with pleasure that his student gave a right answer.

A shimmer! I thanked Phlebas then went through the golden doors and down the grassy hill. For as long as I could will it, I sat at the foot of the hill feeling at one with the three L's of all that is.

An intense shimmer and I was in the Awake World. I said aloud, "My Dream Scene and the Awake World are flip sides of the same coin, with all atoms connected by the three L's."

I grinned. "That's real atomic power!"

On the other side of the golden doors, Phlebas also smiled.

CHAPTER 16

A Hawk Dream

I scanned for the red-tailed hawk without luck. My dress had cascading waterfalls, and I knew what that meant.

I crossed the meadow to the pond and walked onto flat rocks under the waterfall. Water flowed over and through me. I turned several times, enjoying.

Behind the waterfall was a small cave. A dim light shone down a spiral of stairs at the back. Eagerly, I climbed the stairs and came out onto a ledge high up the mountain.

White mist hid the mountain top above me. I stayed close to the mountain wall and marveled at my Dream Scene below.

Curiosity satisfied; I turned toward the stairs. The opening was gone.

With a cry, the red-tailed hawk appeared across the meadow, gliding toward the mountain, growing bigger and bigger. I pressed my back against the mountain as it landed. The hawk was taller than I was.

The hawk asked how I got there, and I explained about the stairway. "I want to go back, but the stairs disappeared."

The hawk cocked its head. "You found the stairs because you wanted to find me. Now you can't find them because you don't want to leave yet."

"Wrong. I want to leave right now."

No response from the hawk. It was just like Ara and Phlebas waiting for an answer. I asked, "Are you really a hawk?"

"A red-tailed hawk, to be exact," it replied.

"I mean...," I groped for words. "Real hawks aren't as big as you." The hawk said, "I am as big as I want or need to be."

"Oh, I forgot. A dream isn't supposed to make sense."

The hawk cocked its head again. "I make perfect sense. Your job is to understand. So, you want to go back down?" The hawk moved closer to the edge.

"Are you going to let me ride down on your back?" I asked.

"You will get yourself down," the hawk said. "Your intent to find me got you here and your intent to return will get you down."

I stared at the hawk. "I can't fly like you do."

"Stand beside me and focus on where you want to land," said the hawk. "I am NOT going to jump!"

"I didn't ask you to jump. Focus on the spot where you want to be. It's that simple."

I look a few very small steps toward the edge and decided I'd like to be between the pond and the lake. "How do I get there?" I asked. "Keep looking at where you want to land," the hawk repeated.

I did and suddenly felt as light as air. I rose from the ledge beside the hawk, keeping focused on my landing spot. We gently landed on that spot.

Excitedly I asked, "How did I fly like that?"

The hawk said. "Truth has many faces. Even behind a lie you may find a bit of truth."

"If something is real, that's the same as truth, isn't it?" I asked.

Instead of answering, the hawk grew smaller and smaller until it was the size of a hawk in the Awake World. "Which is my true self," it asked, "my large image or my small one?"

"It doesn't matter," I said. "This is only a dream. You won't be real when I wake up."

"What if I'm hawk that flies in your Awake World?" Confused, I said nothing.

The hawk asked, "In your Awake World, does everyone see everything in exactly the same way?"

"Of course not," I answered.

"Then what is truth if everyone sees the same thing differently?" asked the hawk.

"Do you mean that what I think is truth is only my truth," I asked, " and that everyone else has their own different truth?"

I imagined millions of people inside the bubble of their own reality floating about Earth with each claiming to have the only truth.

I explained my thought to the hawk, and it nodded. "No wonder the Awake World is such a mess," I said.

I asked how those differences about truth can be fixed. With a few strong wing beats it flew toward the mountain and called back, "You know the answer."

I crossed the meadow and said to myself, "I can't change how others see things, so I'll just send Love and Light to all of them in their separate realities. In my reality I will see Light and Love everywhere, even in their reality."

The golden doors shimmered as I passed through. I ran down the grassy hill, pleased to finally have found the hawk.

I slipped into the Awake World thinking, "I know why the hawk is red-tailed! Red is for love and that hawk sure loves truth.

"It will be fun sending Love and Light to the millions of people in their bubbles. Yes, I love my reality!"

A Lake Dream

I pushed open the golden doors and stepped onto the meadow. Butterflies flew among the flowers on my dress.

ZsuZsu was on the flat, gray rock by the lake. Suddenly the rock was white and so was her long robe. I crossed the meadow to the lake.

"Greetings," she said, giving me a hand up to join her.

Now my dress was white, too. "ZsuZsu," I said. "What kind of dream is this when my dress keeps changing?"

She smiled. "The changes show changing thoughts. This is a lake dream so let's go."

I knew I could breathe dream water as easily as breathing air, so with my hand in hers when ZsuZsu said, "Jump," I did.

We splashed into the water and floated down to the lake bed. Our dresses were blue, and the lake surface was about 20 feet above us.

"The name of this lake is Am," ZsuZsu said. "It mirrors your thoughts."

At her words, the water reflected ZsuZsu and me. "It's like a fun house mirror," I exclaimed.

ZsuZsu smiled. "The Lake of Am isn't always fun." I groaned. "Not a bad dream, I hope."

"That's up to you," she replied with a tilt of her head, then continued. "The Lake of Am reflects thoughts and memories. Remember something you have seen or done."

That was easy. I thought about the first time I stood in the meadow looking around at my Dream Scene.

Now reflections of what I'd seen were around me. The open door of the cottage reminded me of my recent visit to a friend. She had seen me coming and opened the door before I could knock. In the reflection was my friend, laughing at my surprise.

This mirror game was fun, but where was I in the picture? At that thought, ZsuZsu and I were alone in the reflection.

ZsuZsu asked, 'What's the worst thing that could happen to you?" "I can't know what's worse before things happen."

ZsuZsu suggested, "Then imagine being alone and lost in a strange city." Immediately, I was on a city street with strangers walking by looking at me with shifty, narrowed eyes.

It reminded me of my recent Awake World dream about being alone in a town at night where I walked past homes with lighted windows. Families were inside their homes, but I had nowhere to go.

Another Awake World dream: On a street at night, with only one store open; a shadowy figure came at me, and I put my hands out to push the figure away. I couldn't see my hands.

Immediately I was back beside ZsuZsu at the bottom of the Lake of Am. "That wasn't real," ZsuZsu said, "but it felt real, didn't it? Why would you want to experience such fear when it wasn't real?"

"Because you told me to," I snapped back. This lake dream definitely was not fun.

ZsuZsu said, "What same thing happened in every scene?" I didn't know.

"It's the same thing that happens when you are lost in mulling over the past or worrying about the future." ZsuZsu finished. "...YOU disappear."

She was right. My scary dream ended when I couldn't see my hands. I wasn't in any of the reflections. Why?

ZsuZsu explained. "When you are lost in thoughts of the past or future, you are not in the present moment. At that moment you don't exist."

My eyes widened.

She said, "The Lake of Am teaches us to stay in the present moment. Otherwise, we become lost in the unreal zone of past or future, lost to the reality of the present moment. The past and future have their uses, but what kind of a life would you have if most of the time you were as unreal as your daydreams?"

I laughed. "What you just said is as deep as the Lake of Am. Why does that happen?"

"The immediate moment is real," said ZsuZsu. "In unreal zones of past or future, you are no more real than your thoughts. Those thoughts disappear when you come back to the present moment. That's true both in the Lake of Am and in the Awake World."

That idea needed testing. I thought about a fireworks display I'd seen. Instantly fireworks appeared all around us and sure enough, I was gone from the reflection. As soon as I realized this, the fireworks disappeared, and I was back in the reflection beside ZsuZsu.

I chuckled. "So here I am in the Lake of Am."

"Very good," said ZsuZsu. " Always remember to BE wherever you are. Visit the past or future, but don't stay lost in either one."

She gestured and wide golden steps to the surface appeared. "You go first," she said.

I climbed the stairs. When I stepped onto the grass both ZsuZsu and the golden steps were gone. The Lake of Am was perfectly smooth and again the large flat rock was gray.

I crossed the meadow thinking about what ZsuZsu said: "The past and future are in the unreal zone and the only reality is the present moment." The grassy hill shimmered. My dream was ending.

As I slid into the Awake World, I thought, "While I was dreaming, the Awake World didn't exist for me and in a few moments my Dream Scene will be gone when I awake.

"So which one is real? Wherever I am?"

CHAPTER 18

A Woods Dream

I walked through the golden doors and to the woods, the only unexplored place in my Dream Scene.

Birch and banana trees grew side by side, plus plum and pine, mango and apple trees and other unusual combinations. Ferns, blueberry bushes and hazelnut bushes grew between the trees. Interesting.

The flowers usually didn't live together either: Buttercups, orchids, carnations, magnolias, daisies, honeysuckle, roses, dandelions, lotus and others. Their mixed fragrance was so thick and rich I could almost taste it.

Small translucent ovals with wings flitted about. "Those aren't fairies," I said. A ripple of giggles followed my comment.

"We can be fairies if you wish," one said, and the winged ovals took on the appearance of translucent fairies.

"Who are you?" I asked.

A fairy answered, "Call us Little Ones." Another titter. 'We help things here grow." "We have always been in your woods."

I asked, "How can different kinds of trees grow together like this?" The response, "Trees show your abilities, your talents."

So many trees, large and small? I said, "I can't have that many abilities. No way."

One of the Little Ones flew forward. "Don't be offended, but some people have much bigger woods with many other kinds of trees."

That was a good dose of humility.

Little Ones spoke in a rush, but one at a time. "We're glad you came." "Come look around."

I followed them and soon was surrounded by deer and foxes, hummingbirds, woodpeckers and others. A dragonfly flew past.

I stopped. In front of me a big spider web sparkling with dew stretched between two trees. A large spider sat on the web.

"I don't like spiders, so why is it here?" I asked.

A Little One suggested, "Maybe Spider invites you to get closer to nature." From another, "Spider says you can spin ideas into reality." "Dewdrops are treasures."

A Little One suggested, "Maybe Spider invites you to get closer to nature." From another, "Spider says you can spin ideas into reality." "Dewdrops are treasures."

We were joined by an elephant and a mountain lion. A squirrel leaped onto the shoulder of a brown bear that was eating juicy plums.

"I don't remember choosing them," I said, "so why are they here?" "More questions," a Little One said with a giggle. "Maybe you chose the meaning of the animals first." "You need to know your animals." "They teach you many things."

"How do I choose meanings?"

A Little One said, "Squirrel wants you to prepare for the unexpected and to balance work and play." "Bear wants you to stand tall in confidence and strength."

Nearby a woodpecker drummed. A Little One said, "Woodpecker echoes Earth's heartbeat." A robin sang. A Little One said, "Robin sings about happiness with all its heart."

"Mountain Lion says to have courage in life's trials." Another added, "Old Elephant teaches wisdom and kindness."

A penguin waddled by. I laughed and said, "This is fun even if it doesn't make sense."

"It makes good sense," said a Little One. "Penguin wants you to be creative in using your abilities and enjoying life."

The Little Ones flew ahead to a clearing with a ring of darker grass. A fairy ring! They were excited. "Stand in the middle."

"Think of a question." "Listen for the answer." "The answers are inside you."

I couldn't already have answers inside me so asked a question I couldn't possibly answer. I said, "When am I going to die?"

The Little Ones dashed about, agitated. None of them spoke so I asked, "Well, how much time do I have left?" I knew I was being a smart aleck.

Elephant stood in front of me. "You thought you asked an impossible question," it said quietly, "but the answer is truly within you. Your inner wisdom blocks the answer."

Then Elephant raised its trunk and rested it lightly on my shoulder. "Would your knowing that answer make your life better?"

I was ashamed of my attitude.

"I am an Elephant, and I intend to be the best Elephant I can be. That's more important than knowing when we die."

Elephant told me, "Walk through your woods often. Sit in the circle and listen to answers within you. We are your friends and will help you."

I put my arms around its trunk. "Thank you, Elephant," I said and also thanked the other animals, birds and Little Ones.

A shimmer. Everyone came to the edge of the shimmering woods to say goodbye. As I slid into the Awake World, I chuckled. 'There is so much to think about from this dream that it could take me the rest of my life to figure it out."

Then I remembered. "I can go back to the woods and get help whenever I need it. Elephant promised."

CHAPTER 19

A Friends Dream

At the foot of the grassy hill lay a piece of paper with question marks on it. What did that mean? Maybe the answer was in my desk folders. I hurried through the golden doors to the cottage.

I set the folders on the desk and white mist formed inside the wooden frame. Through the mist came Ara, Phlebas and ZsuZsu.

They sat at the long table to my left. Phlebas said, "We came to introduce you to some friends who can join you in future dreams."

Through the mist stepped a man, confident and strong. He sat in the last chair on the left. "Greetings. I am Demosthenes. Do you know of me?"

"Of course, "I answered. "You developed your speaking voice by practicing with pebbles in your mouth to speak louder than the ocean's roar."

Demosthenes laughed. "When I was young, I had shortness of breath and an unpleasant voice that needed training.

"Speaking over the sound of the ocean is symbolic," he said. "Think of the pebbles in my mouth as problems preventing clear speech. I overcame problems with persistence."

I looked at the folders. The top one had his name on it and inside was the explanation he had just given.

Mist formed in the frame and a vibrant woman with expressive dark eyes stepped through. "Hi, everybody. I'm Edie. Rhymes with 'indeedy.' I came to tell you about the big job I have ahead of me." She sat at my right.

"Hi, Edie," I said. "You look familiar."

Long dimples creased her cheeks. "You'll see a lot of me as I poke and prod you whenever you needlessly criticize yourself. My job is to help you gain self-confidence."

I must have had an 'Oh, no!' expression. She added, "Don't look so grim. I've been around, but now you'll hear my advice when you belittle yourself.

Edie continued. "Nobody is better, and nobody is less. I'm here to help you love and accept yourself, Kiddo, and I intend to do just that." Her eyes twinkled with fun and mischief as she sat at my right.

"Thanks," I said, and put her folder in the drawer.

I read "Michelangelo" on the next folder. A bearded man stepped through the mist and sat two chairs down from Edie. The chair between them was too high for an adult.

"I beg your pardon," I began, "but I'm not skilled in the arts, so..."

Michelangelo interrupted, "Enjoying the arts is also a skill. You write poetry and so do I."

I frowned. "I couldn't make poetry or painting my profession, and architecture is way over my head."

He smiled. "My unfinished projects didn't make me a failure. I planned a great tomb with 40 marble statues and didn't finish. St. Peter's Church – the dome was unfinished when I died."

"But your inventions were great," I protested. "Your ideas about flying were ingenious."

Michelangelo nodded. "The creative process invigorates when ideas flow through the brain. My failures taught what I needed to learn in order to create my successes."

"Hello!" A little girl jumped through the frame. "HELLO," we echoed.

Her long coppery hair flipped from side to side as she skipped over to the chair beside Edie.

"I'll help you, kitten," said Edie, and lifted the child onto the higher chair. The girl introduced herself. "I'm Ana and I'm seven." She looked at us. "We are a nice family."

My eyebrows went up. "I thought we were friends."

"Sure," Ana said. "Stuff that flows between our atoms connects us and makes us family. Friends is even better."

She gave me an impish glance. "I'd like to visit your woods sometime so my fairies can meet yours."

A burly young man stepped through the mist. He sat by Michelangelo in the last of the eight chairs.

"I am Angus," he announced.

"Angus?" I repeated. I thought of the bull on my grandparents' farm and tried not to smile.

"Yes. I am the god of love," he said.

This time I did smile. He looked more like a tough warrior. "How can you be the god of love?" I blurted.

"I'm the Celtic god of love," he confirmed. "I can help you learn about love and about appearances being deceiving." This time he was the one who smiled.

Angus asked, "You know about love, don't you?"

This time I was ready. "Love is the Light and Life that fills and connects all of us." Ana gave a nod of agreement.

"Good," said Angus. "One day we will talk about using Love to help others, even those who don't like us."

The frame misted and out stepped a young man in medieval garb holding a stringed instrument. "There are no more chairs," I thought.

"I came to close this session with a song I wrote," he an-nounced. He strummed a few chords then began:

Once on a time I came upon a child so sweet and fair.

My heart was filled with happiness to be with that child there.

The child, the child, I love that child so wonderful and free.

The child, the child, I love that child. Who can that child be?

What joy to know that happy child is the child inside of me.

The child, the child is me.

He doffed his plumed hat and turned, disappearing through the frame. One by one, everyone said goodbye. Last to leave was Edie, who carried Ana. "Do what his song says," Edie told me, "and love that child who is you." Edie, Ana and I shared a three-way hug and, as they stepped into the mist, Ana called back, "I love you."

The last folder on my desk was labeled 'Wandering Minstrel" and his song was inside. "Your song is a keeper," I said.

The room shimmered and before I could leave the cottage, I slipped out of my Dream Scene and back into the Awake World, happy to have so many good friends – including the child who is me.

CHAPTER 20

A Pink Quartz Dream

I fought off the sinking feeling I'd had since watching television news about the hurricane. Thousands of people lost homes, family and friends.

My pink quartz crystal was in my hand because I'd been holding it in the Awake World. I walked up the hill and through the golden doors.

My Dream Scene was silent. No birds sang. The waterfall was frozen in mid splash. Butterflies hid. I crossed the meadow to the garden and sat on a marble bench with a sigh.

"Your sad spirit has affected your Dream Scene," said ZsuZsu coming around the bench. She put her arm around my shoulders.

I explained the tragedy in the Awake World. "The storm is awful, and the people are so scared."

Suddenly I stood and pointed. "Look! Even the Lake of Am is stormy!" The water was rough with whitecaps, flooding onto the meadow.

ZsuZsu took my hand. "Remember the *Rule of the Dreamer* to control the action of a dream? You need to quiet yourself." She told me to close my eyes and take slow, deep breaths.

"Breathe golden-white light into your head, filling all of yourself with Love, Light, Peace and Joy in every breath," said ZsuZsu.

Her hand in mine was reassuring. I closed my eyes and breathed slowly and deeply.

When I opened my eyes, the Lake of Am was mirror smooth.

"Thanks, ZsuZsu," I said. "I do feel better." I described the news coverage of hurricane destruction.

"I saw a little girl standing by herself with both fists pressed on her cheeks.

Her eyes were wide with fear, and nobody paid any attention to her," I said. "Nobody comforted her." Tears stung my eyes as I gripped my pink crystal.

"Would you like to help the child?" ZsuZsu asked. "Sure, but I'm too far away."

ZsuZsu said, "Bring the little girl here to your Dream Scene and comfort her."

I hadn't thought of that. I sat straighter with anticipation. "She was about three or four years old, with curly blonde hair."

ZsuZsu advised, "Imagine her smiling and happy, exactly the way you want her to be."

I did and a moment later the little girl in a pink dress came around the fountain toward me and ZsuZsu.

I held my hands out to her. "I'm glad you came," I said and told her my name. "My friend is ZsuZsu. What is your name?"

"They call me Pinky because that's my most favorite color. I like pink everything." She looked at my crystal. "That's pink. What is it?"

"It's my pink quartz crystal. Do you like it?"

Pinky ran her fingers over the faceted surface. "Oh, yes! It's beautiful." "Why don't you show Pinky the pond," suggested ZsuZsu.

"May I go in the water?" Pinky asked.

"Sure," I said and set my crystal on the bench. "The pond is shallow."

Hand in hand, we crossed the meadow. Butterflies flew up from the flowers and birds sang. My smile was as wide as Pinky's. We stepped into the water with the silky sand between our toes.

Little colored fish bumped our legs as they swam by. Neither of us mentioned the hurricane.

After a bit, Pinky yawned and rubbed her eyes.

"I have a rocking chair in the cottage," I told her. 'Would you like to sit in my lap while I rock and sing to you?"

"Yes! Yes!" she cried, and we headed for the cottage. To my surprise, a pink Christmas tree stood in the corner across from the rocker. It was covered with twinkling pink lights and under it was a soft pink teddy bear.

"May I hold the bear?" Pinky asked. With Pinky in my lap cuddling the teddy bear, we rocked and gazed at the twinkling lights.

The clicking rhythm of the rocker kept time as I made up a little song for her. "Pinky, I love you. I love you so. Pinky, I love you more than you know." Then I sang every happy child's song I could remember.

Pinky's eyes closed. I carried her to the bed and gently set her and the teddy bear against the soft pillows. I kissed her forehead and quietly left.

I joined ZsuZsu in the garden and picked up my pink quartz crystal. "Does Pinky in the Awake World feel better now?" I asked.

ZsuZsu nodded. "You helped her very much even though she won't remember being here in your Dream Scene. Your love is definitely now part of her."

Then ZsuZsu asked, "How do you feel?"

I hadn't been thinking about myself and was surprised that my fearful feelings were gone. "I'm happy," I said and gave ZsuZsu a hug.

"Remember," she told me, "this works in the Awake World, too. Anytime you do something to ease someone's sorrow or pain, you feel better, too."

My Dream Scene began to shimmer. I hurried across the meadow and waved to ZsuZsu. "Thanks, from Pinky and me," I told her.

As I slipped into the Awake World still holding my pink quartz crystal, I imaged Love and Light around people in the storm area, especially dear little Pinky.

"I will never forget you, Pinky," I thought. Then I remembered the wandering minstrel's song about "...the child who is me," and smiled because the child who is me was now wearing a pretty pink dress, just like Pinky's.

CHAPTER 21

Dream-Crafting

I was surprised to see Phlebas at the bottom of the grassy hill. He said, "Your old Dream Scene is gone, and you will craft a new one."

"My Dream Scene is gone?"

Phlebas nodded and gestured toward the top of the hill. There were no golden doors in the mist and no crystal steps.

"Can I really make a new Dream Scene?" I asked.

"You can create any Dream Scene you want, even your old one." "I hope I can," I said.

"You can," he responded. "First, we'll clarify your energies." Streams of light appeared, like Northern Lights dancing on the grass.

"Go into it as though it were the waterfall," he told me.

I stepped into the streams of light-electric violet, green and blue. The colors moved around and through me.

Phlebas said, "The light is cleansing your energy."

"Cleansing it of what?" I asked.

"Negative thinking makes what I call dark dust." He laughed. "You are 'dusting' yourself. The light takes the negative dust particles deep into the Earth where Earth energy changes them back to particles of light."

I felt sparkly tingles all through me. Phlebas said, "That's your empty spaces being filled. Remember when the fear-eating tree took away your fears? The space was filled with…" his voice trailed off.

"With Love," I answered, stepping out of the streaming light.

Phlebas nodded and asked what I would like in my new Dream Scene.

"A cabin by the lake like my uncle's," I quickly said. "How will I get through the mist?"

Phlebas replied, "Imagine any opening you wish." Then he was gone.

"I hope this works," I muttered and imaged a hole in the wall of mist. A dark opening appeared. "But I want the crystal steps back," and there they were.

"So that's how it works. Then I'd rather have the golden doors." There they were.

I waved to the earth beings as I walked up the crystal steps. Pushing open the golden doors, I faced a dark, empty area.

I thought about blue skies and instantly the sky was blue and bright. The vast area of nothing was surrounded by walls of white mist.

As soon as I remembered the woods by the lake, I was standing on a sandy path bordered by pine trees.

Edging the trail were pink bell flowers. I started down the trail. Birds sang and a squirrel on a branch flicked its tail. Several rabbits hopped by.

The trees were so tall that only patches of sky showed overhead. The trail ended at more empty space. "A small, friendly lake is needed," I said. There it was, longer from east to west. I looked down the hill that sloped to the sandy beach.

"A cozy cabin," I said and a neat log cabin was in place.

In this Dream Scene, I wanted daytime sunshine, with stars and moon at night. A sun began shining and white puffy clouds floated by.

"The lake is almost like the Lake of Am," I said and imaged a white rowboat on shore so I could cross the lake where I pictured deer, brown bears and mountain lions, all friendly and waiting for me.

The cabin logs were neatly dovetailed. On the cabin I imaged wide double doors on the south side, with a large deck under an extended roof. The cabin had one room like the cottage in my old Dream Scene.

On the right side of the room, I pictured a writing desk, bookcases and an antique trunk. "It will be fun discovering what's in them."

Soon I had a cupboard, a round oak table with chairs and a large window overlooking the woods. On the table was a plate of cookies. What kind were they? Tasting would have to wait.

As soon as I thought about a stone fireplace on the west side of the cabin, there it was with flames leaping on several logs. "These logs will never burn up so there will be no wood cutting and no ashes," I declared.

Soft scatter rugs were on the wood floor with recliners and rockers in front of the fireplace. Now Phlebas, Ara and ZsuZsu could visit.

I went outside. The sun was setting behind rosy-gold clouds. A full moon rose among the stars. "If only my friends from the old Dream Scene could see this."

"We will come whenever you wish." ZsuZsu said. With her were Ara and Phlebas. "See how easy it is to create a Dream Scene? You did a great job," he complimented me.

Ara said, "This is a beautiful place for new experiences and new friends."

I thought how little Ana would enjoy the lake and animals – and there she was, holding Edie's hand, her eyes wide with childish wonder.

"Maybe Michelangelo will come to paint the scenery," I joked.

"I would love to paint here." Michelangelo was standing on the cabin deck. "I could paint the colorful energy patterns around animals, plants and people." Ana let go of Eddie's hand and went over to him. "I'd like if you painted my picture, too." she said.

Michelangelo scooped her up exuberantly. "Sweet one," he told her, "you will be a delightful subject with the colors of your beautiful thoughts swirling around you."

"Look," said Edie, pointing to greenish Northern Lights dancing in the starry sky. Suddenly my Dream Scene shimmered. My dream was ending.

Everyone chorused, "Goodbye! See you later!" They left, but I still felt the 'hues of love' they had given me.

I slipped into the Awake World knowing I could create any Dream Scene I wanted. How about an old castle?

Anything was possible, but for now I could hardly wait to go back to explore my new cabin and lake.

I wonder what kind of cookies are on that plate?

Rules for the Dreamer

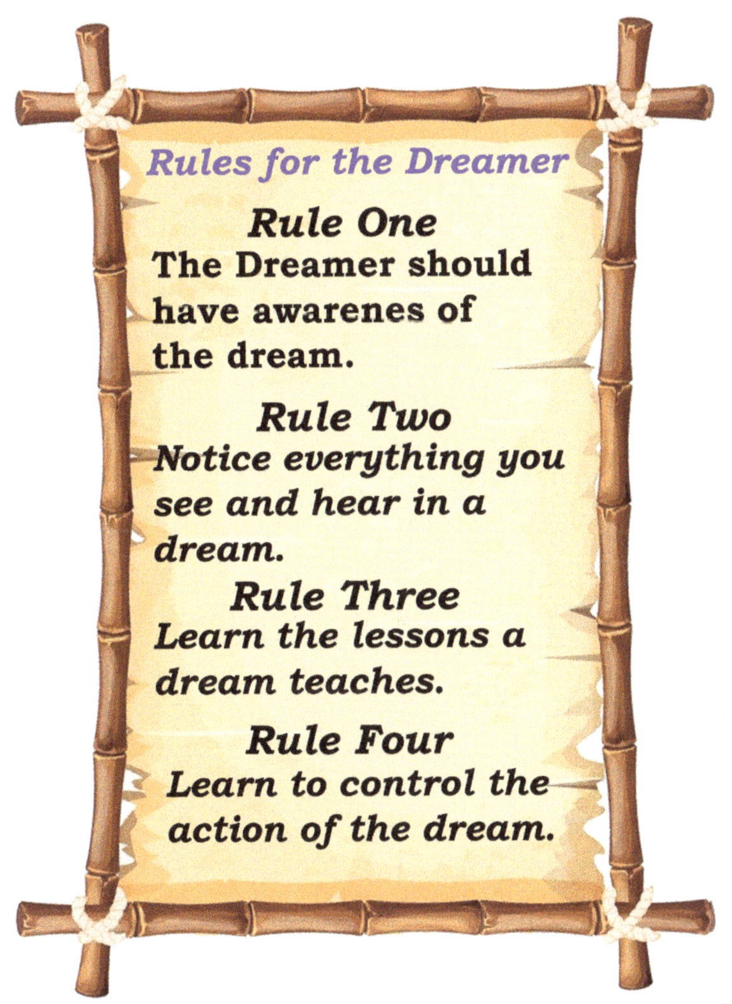

"Blue Angel" Watercolor

Painting by Doreen Lindahl – 1/1/1973

Doreen Lindahl

For years, Doreen worked as a columnist and editor for the *Hibbing Daily Tribune* (now *Mesabi Tribune*). She also published a compilation of poems titled, "I Would Rather Write Than Eat." In 2009, she was awarded the Senior Poet Laureate prize for the state of Minnesota.

Having grown up on the Iron Range in Minnesota, she lived there her entire life until 2021 when she came to live with her daughter in Woodland Park, CO at the age of 92. She loves life in the mountains and her goal is to make it to 100. She is an avid reader and spends her days reading and doing jigsaw and word search puzzles.

Doreen received the nickname "Dorita" from a pen pal in Ecuador in the 1970s named Valdez. He said that was how her name translated in his country. In Spanish, adding 'ita' is a term of endearment.

In 1973, Doreen was driving home from a camp for youth with hearing disabilities. Inspired by the happy atmosphere of the camp, she pulled over by the side of the road to pen these words:

I WISH I KNEW
by Doreen Lindahl

I wish I knew what I could do
To make the world a better place.
To bring a song to every heart
And a smile to every face.

If I had endless money to
Give to those in need,
Or if I had special talents,
I would share them, yes, indeed.

But I am ordinary.
All I have to give
Is the love God put within my heart
When he gave me this life to live.

I will love and live and live in love.
This is all that I can do.
But living love is special work
That can make me happy, too.

I will love and live, and live in love,
And everyone will see

What a better place a little love
Can make the world to be.

Doreen is anything but ordinary! She has indeed shared her special talents and makes the world a better place. In the 1980s, she wrote the lyrics to a song about Dr. Seuss, inspiring local governments across the state to proclaim his birthday as Dr. Seuss Day. She then wrote the man himself a story and sent it to him. He replied with a personal thank you note and a drawing of the Cat in the Hat.

Doreen loves to infuse her writing with fun and humor. Below is from a poem she wrote in 2004 when someone asked, "Aren't you going to write a poem today?"

DISCOVERY
by Doreen Lindahl

I made a big discovery when I
Looked inside my head and
Saw that it was empty;
To myself I said,

"All my words have been used up
So I cannot write a verse ...

But I'm so smart in my old age
That I grabbed the evening paper
And began to eat a page.

I chewed it well and ate some more;
I ate the comics, ads and news
'Till I was full of words again
From my bangs down to my shoes.

Once more my head was full of words,
But I hadn't stopped to think

Doreen enjoyed a second career working at a Health Food Store in Minnesota and retired from that when she turned 80. She has always been health aware and to this day takes no medication. She does a 15-minute chair Pilates exercise program every day. Her attitude is always positive with a smile on her face.

When she was in Minnesota, she became isolated, especially with COVID. All her friends had passed on. So her new life in Colorado is truly a new life for her and she is thankful for every moment...

*Count as precious every breath
That sustains us until death.
Each breath is moved by winds of change
That nurture, balance, rearrange...
Of all the treasures the Earth does hold,
Each breath has value more than gold.*

Breath by Doreen Lindahl

Acknowledgements / Credits

Donna Lindahl St. Dennis — Daughter providing many years of inspiration and encouragement. The big push behind the successful publishing of this book.

Diann Lindahl Pritchard — Daughter who graciously provided me a safe place to live in Colorado after I left Minnesota at the age of 92.

Dave Carlson — Creating the concept, design, and development of the author website (www.d-lindahl.com). Also, many thanks for manuscript layout and editing, image selection, publishing setup, and many behind-the-scenes contributions.

MANY TALENTED ARTISTS PROVIDED IMAGES TO ILLUSTRATE THIS BOOK.

Front Cover: Book with sparkles
       [Thomas Soellner / Shutterstock #1238699236]
Back Cover: Author photo
       [Diann Pritchard]
Chapter 1: Double Golden Doors
       [Filmlandscape / Shutterstock #123662446]
Chapter 1: Woman Resting on Pile of Pillows
       [Irkhamster Stock / Shutterstock #2200341387]
Chapter 1: Grassy Hill in Mist
       [Ryzhkov Oleksandr / Shutterstock #2404742577]
Chapter 2: Red-Tailed Hawk on Branch
       [Daniel Eskridge / Shutterstock #118407946]
Chapter 2: Drums
       [Koba Anastasia / Shutterstock #206371135]

Chapter 2: Yellow Butterflies
[Vicgmyr / Shutterstock #2187714635]
Chapter 3: Strawberry Heart
[Nataliia K. / Shutterstock #517889236]
Chapter 3: Lake Sandy Bottom
[Suppapong L. / Shutterstock #664255006]
Chapter 4: Yellow Cottage
[Popova Valeriya / Shutterstock #124410559]
Chapter 4: Parchment Background ("Rules for the Dreamer")
[Alyona Zhitnaya / Shutterstock #2408254615]
Chapter 4: Red-Tailed Hawk on Branch (end of chapter)
[Daniel Eskridge / Shutterstock #118407946]
Chapter 5: Orange Orb
[Bolbik / Shutterstock #2506120559]
Chapter 6: Philosopher Standing [Anton
Krisnan / Shutterstock #2358005307]
Chapter 6: Green Medallion on Silver Chain
[Lal Perera / Shutterstock #728686831]
Chapter 7: Pink Quartz Crystals
[Yevheniia Rodina / Shutterstock #275049935]
Chapter 7: Pink Chair
[Sene Gal / Shutterstock #87807238]
Chapter 8: Philosopher with Book
[Anton Krisnan / Shutterstock #2359025893]
Chapter 8: Sphere Golden-White Light
[Vector Tatu / Shutterstock #2002822781]
Chapter 9: Angry Woman
[GraphicsRF.com / Shutterstock #2481783639]
Chapter 9: Grocery Checkout Line
[Good Studio / Shutterstock #1154890402]
Chapter 10: White Bag ("Deposit Worries Here")
[Lux Mockup / Shutterstock #1865423887]
Chapter 10: Mirror (rectangular shape)
[Wayne Marques / Shutterstock #59414509]
Chapter 11: Milky Way Galaxy
[NASA Jet Propulsion Laboratory]

Chapter 19: Michelangelo
[doom.ko / Shutterstock #1248786658]
Chapter 19: Singing Minstrel
[Subarashii21 / Shutterstock #2215855249]
Chapter 20: Storm
[Aleksandra Bataeva / Shutterstock #1504936733]
Chapter 20: Pinky
[Yulia Shvetsova / Shutterstock #2390520221]
Chapter 21: Cabin by Lake
[Art4you1 / Shutterstock #2130500975]
Chapter 21: Squirrel on Branch
[Dream Creation / Shutterstock #497215234]
Chapter 21: Cookies on Plate
[Blue Ring Media / Shutterstock #2144391747]
End of Book: Blue Angel
["The Blue Angel": An original watercolor painting by Doreen Lindahl – 1/1/1973]